REMEMBER:

Imagination is the key
to the fairy doors.

JONATHAN b. WRIGHT

Who's Behind
the Fairy Doors?*

*Revised Edition

BY

JONATHAN B. WRIGHT
Certified Fairyologist

Not me!

Illustration by Emma
from page 12 of the
6th journal/guestbook
at Sweetwaters Coffee & Tea

An Urban Fairies™ Book

Published By Urban Fairies Operations, LLC
Ann Arbor, Michigan

www.urban-fairies.com

ISBN13: 978-0-9793585-2-4
Proudly Printed in the United States of America by C-M Books, Inc., Ann Arbor, MI

Who's Behind the Fairy Doors?*

*Revised Edition

Imagination is the key to the fairy doors!™

Sorry, We're CLOSED

BY
JONATHAN B. WRIGHT
Certified Fairyologist

Introduction

In the spring of 2005, I noticed miniature doors - fairy doors - appearing in downtown Ann Arbor. I was already familiar with this phenomenon. In 1993, fairy doors, windows and even rooms and staircases had begun appearing in our home.

I started keeping careful record of my discoveries: I placed journals at the fairy door sites inviting kids and grown-ups alike to write and draw about these urban fairies. As I have never seen a fairy and can only imagine them, I feel fortunate to tap into the creative notions and insights of others.

After careful study of over sixty journals, I have come to the conclusion that children between the ages of 3 and 11 are the most prolific fairy spotters. I share a small portion of the kids' drawings and my augmentations with you now.

I attempted to remain as faithful as possible to the original drawn observations. However, a child's ability to translate their impression to paper is at once both more and less "accurate" than an adult's. A child has less inhibition but perhaps, less technical skill than an adult. I freely acknowledge that my augmentation is neither better nor more precise than the original. Perhaps together we will see a bit more clearly the ever changing world of the imaginary.

My family has helped in the fairy door research. We are working on several books. Visit my website at urban-fairies.com for more information and updates.

Note: None of the children's drawings were damaged in the creation of this book.

FANCY

Remember, *fancy* is in the heart of the believer.

Dear Fairies,
I love you.
I am fancy, too
Eleanor

Illustration by Eleanor
(with dictation assistant)
from page 153 of the
4th journal/guestbook
at the Ann Arbor District Library

Seeing things.

To illustrate my hypothesis of vision versus reality one can look at this illustration of the urban-fairy reading room at the Ann Arbor District Library and a fairy flying by.

You can clearly identify the fairy door and books.
By working in reverse, we can try and render the fairy depicted.

from page 186 of the 2nd journal/guestbook at the Ann Arbor District Library

Same thing... only different.

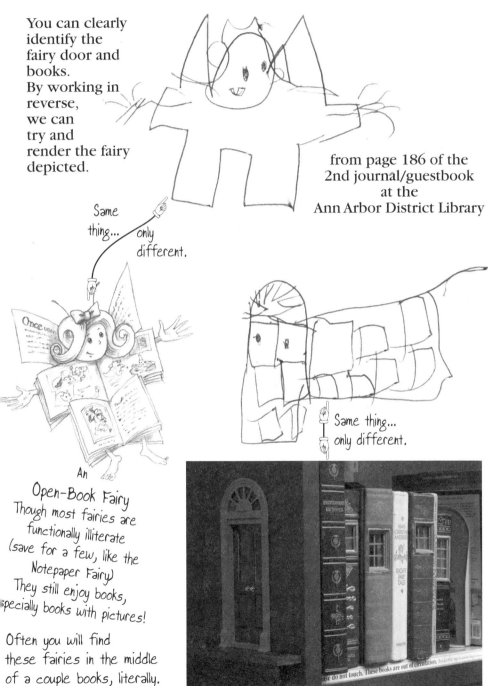

Same thing... only different.

An
Open-Book Fairy
Though most fairies are functionally illiterate (save for a few, like the Notepaper Fairy) They still enjoy books, specially books with pictures!

Often you will find these fairies in the middle of a couple books, literally.

Once upon

3

Illustration by Maddie
from page 54 of the
7th journal/guestbook
at Sweetwaters Coffee & Tea

Where else might one find a
Single-Mocha Fairy
but at a café like Sweetwaters?
There is the lure of baked goods
and, of course the smell of
coffee brewing.

The single mocha fairy is
about 5/8 the size of the
double-mocha fairy and 1/2
the size of a triple mocha.
????
Peculiar mathematics
these fairies have.

Another example of the discrepancy
between the drawing and "reality"
can be seen on these two pages.
Maddie has made an excellent
rendition of the fairy door at
Sweetwaters Coffee & Tea and
the miniature poster. Although her
drawing is lovely, you can see she
employed artistic license.

I will use my own artistic license to try and depict fairies in

this book with enhanced detail.

Illustration by Ashley
from page 64 of the
1st journal/guestbook
at The Peaceable Kingdom
8/27/05

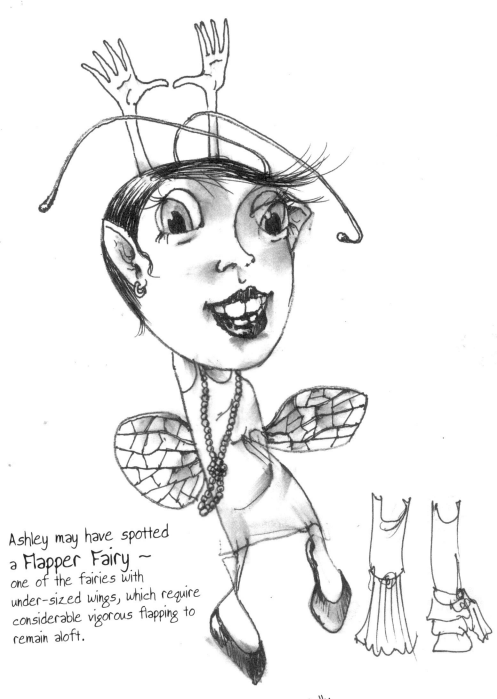

Ashley may have spotted
a **Flapper Fairy** ~
one of the fairies with
under-sized wings, which require
considerable vigorous flapping to
remain aloft.

Coincidentally,
these fairies generally
take their fashion cues
from the so-called "flappers"
of the 1920's.

7

dear fairies,
 are you real?
Is your house
Snuggily?
   Eleanor,
    Age 4

1 6 8 S W 8

Illustration by Eleanor
from page 168 of the
8th journal/guestbook
at Sweetwaters Coffee & Tea

Apparently there are a number of fairies with under-sized vestigial* (or near-vestigial) wings. This fairy has to work pretty hard to get even a few inches off the ground.

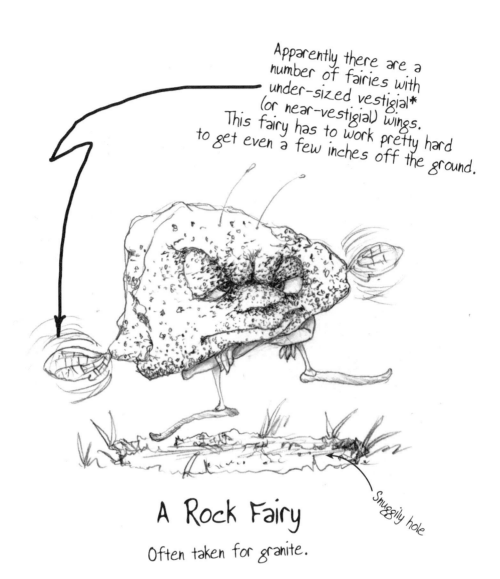

A Rock Fairy

Often taken for granite.

Snuggily hole

Occasionally seen bickering with the Note Paper Fairy & the Scissor-Wing Fairy.

* Vestigial means mostly for show or kinda useless.

Illustration by Cara
from page 40 of the
2nd journal/guestbook
at Sweetwaters Coffee & Tea

0 4 0 S W 2

Looks like a Sanford 0.2mm micro Uni-ball™ roller ball pen.

Old School Notepaper Fairies use feather quills.

11

A Notepaper Fairy
is a type of fairy messenger,
though she is a bit forgetful.

She has a rather large mouth,
but her voice is smallish.

I write my notes on the back of my left hand.

Illustration by Mollie
from page 172 of the
3rd journal/guestbook
at The Peaceable Kingdom

Looks like Mollie has seen a Scissor-Wing Fairy!

It is unclear if these fairies have no hair of their own or shave their heads. However they use their sharpy scissor wings to snip hair from humans and animals and make wigs for themselves.

Illustration by Giulia
from page 6 of the
1st journal/guestbook
at Sweetwaters Coffee & Tea

A Bee-Bottom Fairy

Fairies love trinkets! Luckily, they are quite
elastic as well. This fairy took a fancy to
a metal ring and sqeeeeezed his head right
through to wear as a neck band. I am
pretty sure his body will return to a
normalish shape after it settles a bit.

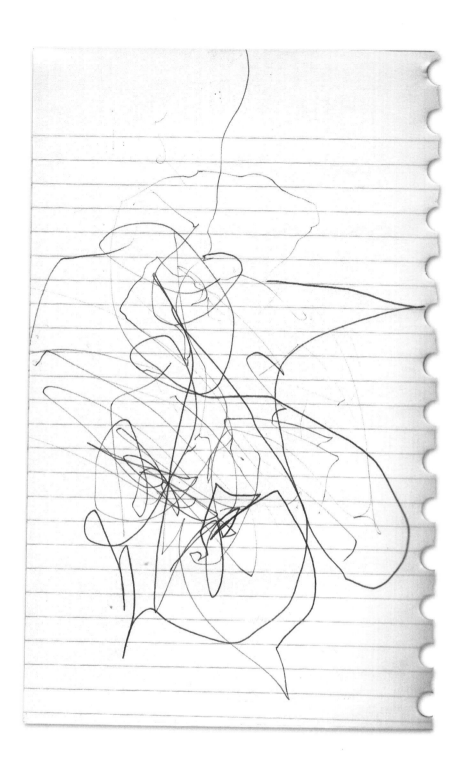

From page 178 of the
1st journal/guestbook
at Jefferson Market

If you have ever seen a sparkler
being waved about on the 4th of July
(VERY carefully, of course),
then you probably have an idea of
what a moving fairy might look like...

... even if you only glimpse the
glowing tips of a very energetic
Sparkling Fairy.

17

Illustration by Hannah
from page 51 of the
5th journal/guestbook
at Sweetwaters Coffee & Tea

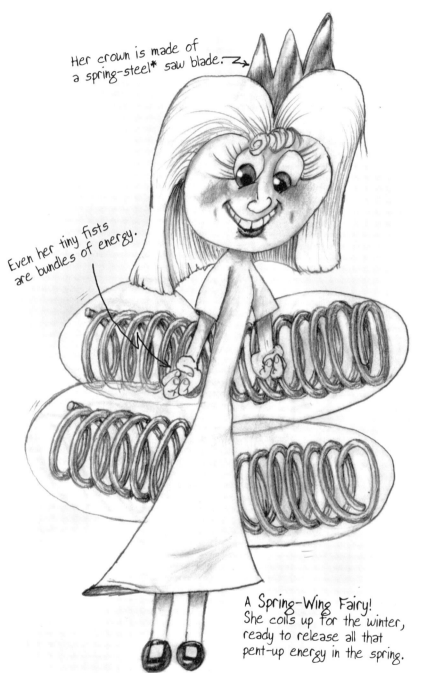

Her crown is made of
a spring-steel* saw blade.

Even her tiny fists
are bundles of energy.

A Spring-Wing Fairy!
She coils up for the winter,
ready to release all that
pent-up energy in the spring.

* Many believe that iron (steel) is toxic to fairies.
From my observations of New World urban fairies,
it is clear that they have somehow built up a tolerance or immunity to iron.

From page 4 of the
3rd journal/guestbook
at Voilà Boutique

Even fairies like to play dress-up & pretend... in this case sqeeeezing into a toiletpaper tube & becoming a super hero!

There seems to be some damage from an encounter with the dread

COMPACTOR!

He would have an unfair advantage with his hands free.

Naturally, we have no idea as to the real identity of this fairy.

21

Special contribution
Illustration by Yuyuko (age 3)

The Burlap-Sack Fairy is unique to the fairy world. Most fairies are happy and carefree, but the Burlap-Sack Fairy tends to worry and fret. His buttons fall off & his outfit frays.

Sadly, this fairy lost a leg to a nasty 'possum.

23

Special contribution
Illustration by Will

A Capsize Fairy
A Capsize's headwear is as large as his body. Of course this can lead to some instability, tipping to port or starboard... or star-ward.

"Capsize" is the word used when a boat tips over.
On a boat, "port" means "left" and "starboard" means "right".

Illustration by Caroline
from page 146 of the
3rd journal/guestbook
at The Peaceable Kingdom

Flying isn't the ONLY way to get around.

OMNI DIRECTIONAL

A Caster-Foot Fairy
Is she bio-mechanical?
Are her rollers prosthetic feet,
or do they slip on
like rollerblades?

Actual size of drawing.

Illustration by Rachel
from page 58 of the
3rd journal/guestbook
at Voilà Boutique

Tinkle Bell Fairy

She is not related to that *other* Bell fairy.
<u>This </u>one is named for the delicate sound she makes
& her distinctive silver dress (?)... outfit (?).

Too often we stereotype fairies as being slight of build. Just like humans, they come in many shapes & sizes. The Tinkle Bell fairy is quite tiny, though not as small as a Mite Fairy.

Actual size of drawing.

Illustration by Rachel
from page 140 of the
2nd journal/guestbook
at Voilà Boutique

A Mite Fairy's wings are nearly transparent. You might just see the outer structure.

You also might make out the bold pattern of her outfit.

A Mite Fairy
is one of the weensiest fairies.

Magnified about 2x *

* Actual size of fairies might vary.

Illustration by Evan
from page 178 of the
7th journal/guestbook
at Sweetwaters Coffee & Tea

33

Illustration by Katy
from page 13 of the
2nd journal/guestbook
at Voilà Boutique

I'm back!

If you happen to see a Boomerang Fairy, and it flies off in its distinctive spinning manner... wait a bit, as it is certain to return.

Stabilizing ears.

Stabilizing winglets.

Obviously Katy has drawn a
Boomerang Fairy.

Illustration by Kaitlyn
from page 29 of the
8th journal/guestbook
at Sweetwaters Coffee & Tea

The **Acrobat-Hat Fairy** is not just ONE fairy but a symbiotic relationship between the "host" fairy and the "hat" fairies.

Although the Acrobats are not exactly a "hat," they are in constant motion, collectively becoming a colorful, kinetic headpiece. Occasionally one may stop to strike a pose.

Unlike the relationship between the Egyptian Plover and the Crocodile, the Acrobats do not seem to serve any function beyond entertainment and perhaps embellishment. Of course, in the fairy world that counts for a lot!

Acrobat-Hat Fairy

Illustration by Lane
from page 52 of the
5th journal/guestbook
at Sweetwaters Coffee & Tea

Much like a beetle, the Mecha Beetle's wings are protected by an outer shell.

Just one antennae!

Specialized needle-like protrusions for landing on marshmallowish surfaces.

A Japanese Mecha-Beetle Fairy

It looks as if this one has lost a contact lens, but that's just silly.

When not flying, the Mecha-Beetle looks very much like a beetle bug.

MOUSIE FAIRY
BY RACHEL
MARTIN

Illustration by Rachel Martin
from page 144 of the
2nd journal/guestbook
at Nicola's Books

Mousie Fairy

Just as the Mecha-Beetle can appear like a beetle and the rock fairy as a
chunk of stone, fairies can use their "fairy glamour" to disappear or
appear as something natural, like a butterfly, a scurrying mouse or a firefly.

41

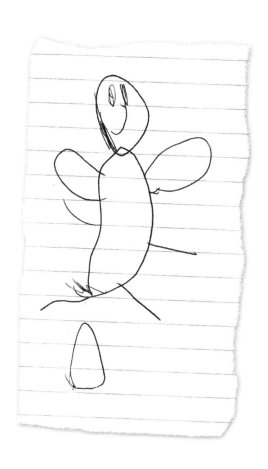

from page 137 of the
1st journal/guestbook
at Jefferson Market

Stunt Fairy

43

He is probably playing
the traditional
fairy rhyme game:

Glik be nimble
Glik be quick
Glik fly over the candycorn

I sure hope that's candy corn.
It looks like candy corn.
I'm sure it is.

Actual size of drawing.

Illustration by Delanie & Jamison
from page 183 of the
1st journal/guestbook
at Voilà Boutique

Another very small fairy shown much larger than the original. The size of a Bubble Fairy may vary with air pressure.

A Bubble Fairy

Because a Bubble Fairy is transparent, it is difficult to see. Like other fairies, the Bubble Fairy can COMPLETELY vanish and when it does there is a distinct "POP!"

Delanie or Jamison has very nice handwriting!

Illustration by Grayson
from page 193 of the
3rd journal/guestbook
at Voilà Boutique

Hairy-Queen Fairy

I'll bet with a name like that, she likes ice cream.

Although many think that a real fur dress would be cruel, the fairies' close association with nature assures that the fur was snipped from willing bunnies... maybe by a Scissor-Wing Fairy?

The furry slippers are artificial.

Actual size of drawing.

Illustration by Stephanie
from page 45 of the
1st journal/guestbook
at Sweetwaters Coffee & Tea

In nature, the male of a species is frequently much smaller than the female.

(For size comparison.)

His antennae have been bent downward by his crown.

King or not, he looks a bit skittish.

Like the Hairy-Queen Fairy, the Hairy-King Fairy also dresses in fur.

Hairy-King Fairy

(Enlarged to show detail.)

49

Drawings reduced to fit.

Illustrations by Amina-age-10
received via e-mail

Amina's drawings are clearly labeled
and require very little enhancement from me, which is
substantiated by the accuracy of the doors and windows.

I chose just one to augment:
the
Voilà Fairy

Unfortunately the boutique,
Voilà, closed. Just before
it did, the fairy door
vanished without a trace.
As far as I know, the
Voilà Fairy has not been
seen since. But just like
magic~
VOILÀ!* she's likely to
reappear right there...

Notice that each fairy
has unique clothing, hair
style & wings...

—— The Ark Fairy even has a microphone, which makes perfect sense as The Ark is a folk music theater.

... or there!

... or there!

51

* "Voilà" means "there" in French.

Illustration by Miss Sierra
from page 112 of the
1st journal/guestbook
at The Peaceable Kingdom

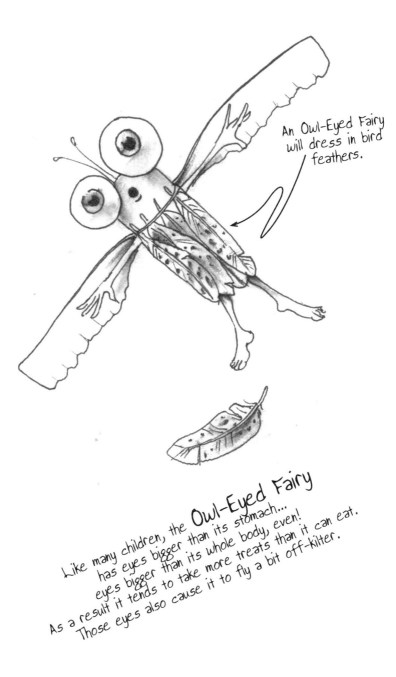

An Owl-Eyed Fairy will dress in bird feathers.

Owl-Eyed Fairy

Like many children, the Owl-Eyed Fairy has eyes bigger than its stomach... eyes bigger than its whole body, even! As a result it tends to take more treats than it can eat. Those eyes also cause it to fly a bit off-kilter.

CHARLIE
AGE 3

Illustration by Charlie
from page 103 of the
8th journal/guestbook
at The Peaceable Kingdom

A Star Swallower Fairy

Have you ever noticed that you cannot see any stars, except the sun, during the day?

A Star Swallower will swallow up loose stars until he cannot hold any more. Then he will spew them back out again. The swallowing tends to happen around dawn and the spewing at about dusk, but some swallowing can happen on cloudy nights as well.

If you ever feel that your "stars are out of alignment," perhaps a star swallower has gulped some down.

vincent age
8

Illustration by Vincent
from page 52 of the
1st journal/guestbook
at Nicola's Books.

The Great Scot Fairy can be recognized by the Rrrrrolling "R" sounds he makes. The great Scot is a story teller who often speaks in hyperbole, which is a sort of language where actual facts may be embellished a bit.*

He has 2 mouths so he can do two characters at once in his stories,

Or add sound effects or even sing while playing the mouse pipes.

ne Great Scot arries a "konker", special airy "Wand". While the Star Swallower makes stars disappear, the konker can make you see stars. The Irish might call konker a shellelagh.

This fella must be friends with a leprechaun, as he is wearing boots; leprechauns are known to be cobblers and Great Scot Fairies typically go barefoot. It seems he has not yet got the knack of laces.

the **Great Scot Fairy** is quite a burly fairy, he is no girly fairy, so do not be fooled by his skirt, that is a kilt.

and that's no purse, that's a sporran, for carrying useful things when your skirt ... er... kilt has no pockets. Ok, it's a purse, but it's a burly sort of purse.

* Perhaps you will hear him tell of how a fearsome beasty clawed his shoulder. Though he was seen flitting awkwardly about the thorny branches of a raspberry bush just a few hours ago.

This page is nearly as wordy as the Great Scot!

57

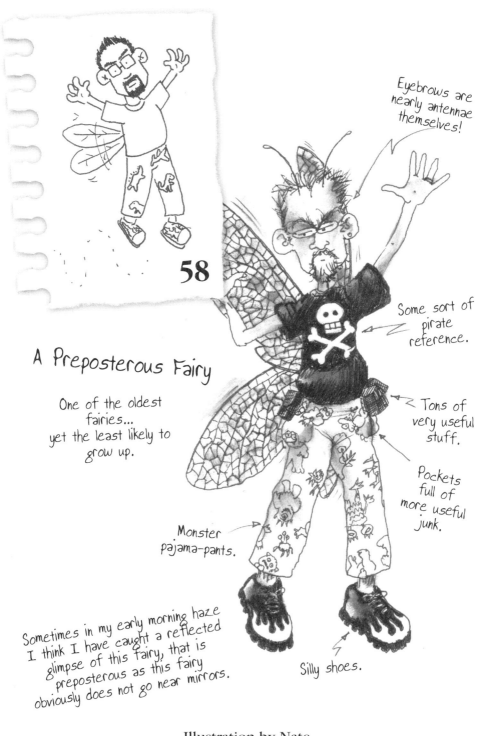

58

A Preposterous Fairy

One of the oldest fairies... yet the least likely to grow up.

Eyebrows are nearly antennae themselves!

Some sort of pirate reference.

Tons of very useful stuff.

Pockets full of more useful junk.

Monster pajama-pants.

Sometimes in my early morning haze I think I have caught a reflected glimpse of this fairy, that is preposterous as this fairy obviously does not go near mirrors.

Silly shoes.

Illustration by Nate
(with Tiffany's consultation)
from page 111 of
the 6th journal/guestbook
Sweetwaters Coffee & Tea

u.f.o.

Some of the Original *Fairy Doors of Ann Arbor & Dexter*

Fairies come and go on a whim. At any given moment a fairy door may be there..... or not.

$\mathcal{M}$any thanks are due to family, friends and people I have never met who have contributed to <u>Who's Behind the Fairy Doors?</u>* Revised Edition.

I thank God for making us in his image, full of imagination; Kathleen, for all of her support and introducing me to her interest in fairies; Samuelina & Delaney, our daughters, who have had brilliant insights and contributions; Tiana four her expret editting. - (heehee), Josh & Phil, for helping to launch Urban Fairies Operations; Colleen, Kellie & Brent for creative and corrective input.

The folk of businesses in Ann Arbor which are or have hosted urban fairies™: Carol, Wei & Lisa and Joan; Elaine & Cynthia; Richard; Catherine; Lori; Jean; Nicola; Mary; Lee Ann; Laura & Tahira.

Of course all the contributing illustrators:
Amina, Ashley, Cara, Caroline, Charlie, Delanie, Eleanor(s), Emma, Emilie, Evan, Giulia, Grayson, Hannah, Jamison, John, Kaitlyn, Katy, Lane, Maddie, Mollie, Nate, Rachel(s), Sierra, Stephanie, Tiffany, Vincent, Will & Juyuko & those who did not or could not sign their names.

This printing was made possible through the pineapple* support of many people:

Lisa and Wei Bee of Sweetwaters Coffee & Tea • Nicola's Books FOUND Gallery • Marci Woolson and Mike Woodgerd • The Peaceable Kingdom • "International Fairy Friendship House" where fairies and wee folk from around the world call in for a cuppa and cake in Beaufort Victoria Australia.

Nicklaus & Pamela and Erica Suino, Steve Wright, Angela Hoffmann, Markus Nee, Dianne Marsh, Debra Freeman, Brad Dancer, Dan Cichoracki, Don and Deb Laneville, Cynthia Akiyoshi, Jody Glancy Scott, Andy & Nicole Cluley, Elise Christle, Margeaux Allen, Swanna C Saltiel, Melinda Porter & Megan Porter, Anne & Rod Shelton, Joan, Julianne Pinsak, Kate Lebowsky, Julie Dutton Sullivan, Jennifer Nast, Claudia and Clark Doughty, Christine Klimek, Laura Hamel, Debby Albert, Paula Lynn, Irene L. Felicetti, Ileana and Jaylee Oeschger, Betty and Patrick Ray, Carol Mulanix Kiple, Jorie Uren, Lynn Holland, Sylvaine Title, Hayley Breines & Sunny, Kathleen Rubert, Eric, Karen A. Chartier, Jonna Asher, Isabella Hoye, "The Ruff House", Michelle W. Nee, Linda J. Spector, Anne, Jennifer S. Pena, Patrice Iacovoni and Joe Morton, Carlton Lemley, Kathy Overington, B.J. Whimpey, Heather McWilliams, Patricia A Beckham, Kellie, Zoe Wright, Jane Thomson Carron (a High School pal who believes in Fairies), Tiffany, Rob & Emily, Jill Valuet, Gryffyn Greene, Kerry MacDonell, Kate Menard, Joseph B. Pomerville, Winifred van Veen-Miller, Kitty B. Kahn, Allen Salyer (Detroit), Daven, DeeDee, Aviva I. Dintenfass, Alexandra Lane, Sonja Biggs, Laura Schirling Laura M., Suzanne Baltrip, Mary Aviles, Rebecca Clarke and Ashleigh Schenk, Talula Marie Pletschoff, Karen Loros, Chris Haddlesey, Ember Hansen, Tosje, The Reed Family, Jayde M Reynolds, Raelynn Beebe, Daniel Winterhalter, Patrick Goussy AND Em Orzol

To Fairy Finders all over, stay fancy my friends.
~ jonathan

* *Pineapple support.*
Okay, this requires a short story to explain:
Delaney, our youngest, when she was much younger, gave a performance which ended with a bow and, "Thank you for your pineapple support." Apparently she had been watching Public Television, which often concludes with "Thank you for your *financial* support."